T3-AME-264

In memory of my Illinois family,
who lived and loved farm life.

My mother and father grew up on small
family farms in Illinois, and
my childhood memories of visits
to those farms have left lasting impressions.

The farm is where I learned to love
the smell of spring rains and
where I became a cloud watcher
while walking through fields of corn on
hot summer days. It is where I learned
to love the land, to love nature,
and to love the animals.

G. P. PUTNAM'S SONS
A division of Penguin Young Readers Group.
Published by The Penguin Group.
Penguin Group (USA) Inc., 375 Hudson Street, New York, NY 10014, U.S.A.
Penguin Group (Canada), 90 Eglinton Avenue East, Suite 700, Toronto,
Ontario M4P 2Y3, Canada (a division of Pearson Penguin Canada Inc.).
Penguin Books Ltd, 80 Strand, London WC2R 0RL, England.
Penguin Ireland, 25 St. Stephen's Green, Dublin 2, Ireland (a division of Penguin Books Ltd.).
Penguin Group (Australia), 250 Camberwell Road, Camberwell, Victoria 3124, Australia
(a division of Pearson Australia Group Pty Ltd).
Penguin Books India Pvt Ltd, 11 Community Centre, Panchsheel Park,
New Delhi - 110 017, India.
Penguin Group (NZ), 67 Apollo Drive, Rosedale, North Shore 0632, New Zealand
(a division of Pearson New Zealand Ltd).
Penguin Books (South Africa) (Pty) Ltd, 24 Sturdee Avenue, Rosebank,
Johannesburg 2196, South Africa.
Penguin Books Ltd, Registered Offices: 80 Strand, London WC2R 0RL, England.

Copyright © 2011 by Wendell Minor. All rights reserved. This book, or parts thereof, may not
be reproduced in any form without permission in writing from the publisher, G. P. Putnam's
Sons, a division of Penguin Young Readers Group, 345 Hudson Street, New York, NY 10014.
G. P. Putnam's Sons, Reg. U.S. Pat. & Tm. Off. The scanning, uploading and distribution of
this book via the Internet or via any other means without the permission of the publisher
is illegal and punishable by law. Please purchase only authorized electronic editions, and do
not participate in or encourage electronic piracy of copyrighted materials. Your support of
the author's rights is appreciated. The publisher does not have any control over and does
not assume any responsibility for author or third-party websites or their content.

Published simultaneously in Canada.
Manufactured in China by South China Printing Co. Ltd.
Design by Marikka Tamura. Text set in Klepto ITC.
The art was created in watercolor gouache on Strathmore 500 bristol 3-ply paper.
Library of Congress Cataloging-in-Publication Data
Minor, Wendell.   My farm friends / Wendell Minor.   p. cm.
Summary: Simple, rhyming text describes the characteristics of different farm
animals. includes "Farm friends fun facts" and books and websites for
further reading. [1. Stories in rhyme. 2. Domestic animals—Fiction.] i. Title.
PZ8.3.M6467My 2011   [E]—dc22   2010014793
ISBN 978-0-399-24477-3
Special Markets ISBN 978-0-399-25578-6 Not for resale
1 3 5 7 9 10 8 6 4 2

This Imagination Library edition is published by Penguin Group (USA), a Pearson
company, exclusively for Dolly Parton's Imagination Library, a not-for-profit
program designed to inspire a love of reading and learning, sponsored in part by The
Dollywood Foundation. Penguin's trade editions of this work are available wherever
books are sold.

My
FARM
FRIENDS

WENDELL MINOR

G. P. Putnam's Sons • An Imprint of Penguin Group (USA) Inc.

WELCOME TO THE FARM

All kinds of animals live on the farm
Some live outside, some live in the barn
Furry ones,
feathered ones,
woolly ones too
Some things that they do
Just might surprise you!

Roosters
crow all day long
They say cock-a-doodle-doo

When it's early in the morning
Will you cock-a-doodle too?

Pigs can't sweat
Or jump in a pool

So they roll in the mud
That's how they stay cool

Billy goat,
silly goat,
chews everything
Just because he's curious
And when he nibbles at your clothes
It might make you furious

Turkeys can be very friendly
Sometimes sitting in your lap
They even purr when they're content
Just like a
kitty cat!

Cats work hard on the farm
Chasing mice from the barn

They also spend much time at rest
Sometimes a lamb's back is the best!

Cows drink a bathtub
full of water
To produce milk every day

But suppose you tried
to take a bath
And a cow got in your way?

Chickens take dust baths
And wear a comb on their head

Chickens come in many colors
But their combs are always red

Sheep are gentle creatures
Who get nervous when alone
But when they find their flock
They feel happy and at home

Horses eat hay
And horses say neigh
They sleep standing up

Could you
sleep that way?

Lots of baby animals
live on the farm too
And guess what—

They would all love to have
A visit from **YOU!**

MY FARM FRIENDS FUN FACTS

 Holstein COWS are black and white, and each has a different pattern. The average cow gives about 8 gallons of milk each day, or 100 glasses of milk! It is believed that cows give more milk when they are called by their names.

 PIGS are very smart and some learn tricks better than dogs. Because pigs can't sweat, they like to cool off in the mud, but otherwise they are very clean creatures. They are very social and often sleep snout to snout.

 There are over 150 types of domestic CHICKENS, and they come in many different colors and patterns. They lay different colored eggs such as white, brown, green, pink and blue. The average hen lays 265 eggs each year.

 SHEEP make a bleating sound, and a baby lamb can recognize its mother by her bleat. When sheep drink, they prefer running water. Sheep are sheared for their wool, and one pound of wool can make ten miles of yarn.

 GOATS are actually picky eaters, but because they are very curious, they nibble at many things, like clothes and cardboard. Baby goats are called kids, and they like to play and jump on top of other animals.

 Like most birds, ROOSTERS are most vocal early in the morning when they greet the rising sun. Roosters crow at other times of the day to protect their hens in the barnyard.

Barn CATS make friends with other farm animals. When looking for a spot to nap, they often choose the back of a sheep, horse or cow. Barn cats are sometimes rewarded for catching mice with a bowl of fresh cow's milk.

 Before they hatch from their shells, baby CHICKS can hear their mother's clucking. It takes 21 days before a baby chick can hatch from its shell. Baby chicks learn from their mothers what food they should and should not eat.

 HORSES really can sleep standing up, and they often do. They belong to the same family of animals that includes zebras, mules and donkeys. Some farm horses are used to pull old-fashioned plows, carriages and sleighs.

 A male TURKEY's gobble can be heard up to a mile away. Female turkeys make a clucking sound, and when relaxed and content, they can make a purring sound. Most farm turkeys are so heavy, they are unable to fly.

Acknowledgments

I would like to thank my friends Michael and Fran Keilty of Maple Spring Farm,
Natalie and Elisha Dyer of Dyer-Need Farm, and Marylou and Bob Bondi of Amber Waves Farm
for so generously allowing me to use their farm friends as models for this book.

Internet Sources

Farm Sanctuary, Watkins Glen, New York • www.farmsanctuary.org
Animal Place Farmed Animal Sanctuary & Education Center • www.animalplace.org
Wrights Dairy Farm & Bakery • www.wrightsdairyfarm.com
Walnut Springs Farm • www.strawberryfarm.com
Farm Animals for Kids and Teachers • www.kiddyhouse.com/Farm
Chickens—Top 10 Facts—University of Arkansas Division of Agriculture • www.kidsarus.org/kids_go4it/growit/raiseit/chickens.htm